Veronica

Franklin
IS MESSY

Franklin is a trade mark of Kids Can Press Ltd.

ISBN 0-590-48686-1

38 37 36   11 12 13 14 15/0

Printed in the U.S.A.   40

First Scholastic printing, November 1994

Franklin
IS MESSY

Paulette Bourgeois • Brenda Clark

SCHOLASTIC INC.
New York Toronto London Auckland Sydney

Franklin could count forwards and backwards. He could zip zippers and button buttons. He could tie his shoes and count by twos. But Franklin was so messy that he could hardly ever find his things. Even special things.

One day Franklin searched for his sword. It was special because he had made it himself from cardboard and wood and string. Franklin needed it to play Knights in Armor with his friends.

He looked all over. He found a bag of marbles he thought he had lost. He found a brown apple core. He even found his favorite baseball hat. But he couldn't find his sword.

"Have you seen my sword?" Franklin asked his mother. Franklin's mother looked around his room. She shook her head. "All I see is a big mess. Please tidy this room before you go out to play."

Franklin muttered to himself. Why all the fuss about a little mess? He had more important things to worry about. He might miss playing Knights.

Franklin hurried. He opened his closet and heaped an armful of books inside. He piled all his blocks in the middle of his room. He threw his hat in the corner and put the apple core in a drawer.

"All done!" he said to himself. Still, he hadn't found his sword.

By the time Franklin reached Bear's house, his friends were already playing Knights. Bear slashed the air with his sword. Beaver lunged at evil dragons.

"Hurry, Franklin!" shouted Bear. "We need you."

"I can't," whispered Franklin.

The game stopped. "Why not?" they asked.

"I don't have my sword," said Franklin.

Bear was disappointed. "But how can we play Knights without swords?" he asked.

Franklin looked around. He found a stick on the ground. "I'll use this," he said.

They fought dragons all afternoon.

"Tomorrow," said Franklin, "I will have my own sword.
Then we can save Lady Beaver from a fire-breathing dragon.
We are courageous Sir Franklin and Sir Bear."

Beaver slapped her tail down — hard. "I don't want
to be saved. I want to be a brave knight, too."

"All right," said Franklin. "You can be Sir Lady Beaver.
And together we will save the king."

"You'll need your special sword," said Bear.

"Of course," said Franklin.

When Franklin got home, his father was annoyed.

"I found this in your drawer," he said, holding the apple core. "That's not where it belongs. And I found this hat on the floor. That's not where it belongs, either."

Franklin threw the apple in the garbage and hung up his hat. Why all the fuss about a little mess?

Goose came by looking for a puzzle she had loaned to Franklin. "Can I please have my puzzle back?" she said.

Franklin looked. His room was such a mess that he couldn't see the puzzle among the books and crayons and blocks.

"Maybe it's in my closet," said Franklin.

Franklin opened the closet door. It was messy in there, too.
He stepped inside.
Crr-uu-nch!
It was a very loud noise.

Franklin's parents came rushing in.
"Are you all right?" they asked.
"I'm all right," said Franklin. "But my sword isn't."
He held up the shattered pieces.
"What a mess!" Franklin said sadly.
"Maybe you need more places to put your things,"
said Franklin's mother.

They found boxes in the basement. They painted them and named them: toy box, puzzle box, costume box, block box. They put books on the bookshelf. Then they put a special hook on the back of the door for a new sword.

The tidying-up took a long time. But it wasn't so bad because Franklin found lots of things he thought he'd lost. Goose's puzzle, his own favorite purple crayon, and enough cardboard, wood, and string to make a new sword and even a shield.

The next morning Franklin dressed in full armor. He was especially proud of his new shield. It said: SIR FRANKLIN. LOYAL AND BRAVE.

"Sir Franklin," said his mother, "I think you forgot something."

Franklin's mother whispered in his ear.

Franklin smiled. They took a crayon and added two more words to his shield.

SIR FRANKLIN. LOYAL AND BRAVE AND NEAT.